The Lighten Your Vibe Coloring Book

Christina Brittain

Balboa Press books may be ordered through booksellers or by contacting:

Balboa Press
A Division of Hay House
1663 Liberty Drive
Bloomington, IN 47403
www.balboapress.com
1 (877) 407-4847

ISBN: 978-1-5043-4872-0 (sc)

Print information available on the last page.

Balboa Press rev. date: 2/26/2016

BALBOA.
PRESS
A DIVISION OF HAY HOUSE

This book is dedicated to the spirit of celebration!

Acknowledgments

It is a breathtaking thing to realize how MANY angels participated in the creation of this book! And to realize that the book itself called in the perfect and necessary midwives to usher it in!

To my dear circle of friends far and wide, and to my remarkable clients and students, you have loved and encouraged me in countless, beautiful ways. Each of you contributes more love, joy and support than you'll ever know!

To Sunny Sangster, the computer goddess with a heart of gold! You have a true and shining genius, and I'm deeply grateful you blessed this book with it!

To my assistant Erin Brown, your skills and attention are so nuanced, graceful and powerful! I appreciate you with all my heart!

To my soul cousin Katie Autote, thank you for the pics, the playfulness and the deep and enduring friendship. I love you Prima!

To Billie Ann Franchella, thank you for showing up in Maui for our Divine play date! I'm sure the fun we've been having – and have planned – has been in The Works for a while! Thank you for the countless expansive phone calls. And for getting goosebumps when I first told you about the coloring books. I love you so much!

To Lane, Nancy, Allison and Ruth who lent me their fabulous editing skills!

To the flat-out amazing Lane Blake! No words can express how much you have blessed me. I am in awe of your generosity and how MANY ways you have shared your light and talents with me. You were a major catalyst for this project and I am honored that you believed in my work long before the coloring books were even a twinkle in my eye. I love you!

To Nancy O'Fallon, we clearly showed up in each other's lives on schedule! Thank you for your authentic, powerful being and for sharing it with me. I'm so glad we get to journey together!

To Allison Rolfe, honey, you just "get" this book! Probably because the book had you in mind all along! I am moved beyond gratitude for the endless ways you poured love toward me during this entire project. You are an extraordinary being, and it gives me huge joy that you know that.

continued....

To my shaman-mystic-wise-woman friend Ruth Watson, the way you live is mastery. The way you be is a lighthouse. Time and again on this journey it helps point me home to myself and my true frequency. Thank you for the many ways you are so present and loving. Thank you for being so You.

And huge thanks to whatever Loving Force dropped the inspiration for the coloring books into my head! I feel privileged to have been invited into such a radically uplifting project. It has changed me in its brilliant fire of transformation, and given me a sweet and powerful means to share love as only I can.

And to all of you reading this book, thank you from the depths of my soul for all that YOU contribute to Everything, and for effortlessly sharing love as only you all can.

Introduction

Let's say the good stuff! Let's talk about the wonderfulness of the world! Let's name it! Let's say it out loud when we love someone or something. Amazing stuff is going on all the time! Life is extraordinary! We don't have to let it go by without noticing it! We can open our eyes and our arms and receive it – and that's what we're doing every time we talk about it. When we compliment someone or celebrate something we're giving JOY a voice in the world. We are making joy more real for everyone. Give yourself the right to be happy. Give yourself permission to notice all the goodness, and live surrounded by all that love.

When I was a kid I could see that people stopped themselves from saying the good stuff. They didn't like to point out all the wonderful things about themselves – or even about other people. It was obvious to me that not enough compliments and love were being said out loud! I decided I would say it whenever I had a nice thought about someone. I took it upon myself to make that my job! In fact, it became a career! As an Expressive Arts Therapist, intuitive counselor, and now as an inspirational cartoonist, I've always focused on helping people realize how amazing they are!

When I was an Expressive Arts Therapist, I had an office that overlooked a busy intersection. The office had a huge window that commuters couldn't help but notice as they drove by! It was a perfect opportunity to say the good stuff! I put up signs that reminded people that they are wonderful. And that life is beautiful and conspiring in their favor! Many people called to say that the

message I put up that week was exactly what they needed to hear, or to thank me for taking the time to provide ongoing upliftment to the community. My favorite call was from a mother who said she and her daughter passed by the window sign every day as she drove her daughter to school. She asked me if I would please email her a list of every sign I'd ever put in that window, because the messages were sparking meaningful conversations between her and her daughter. I loved that the window signs were literally helping people talk about positive ways to see themselves and the universe we live in!

Eventually I moved out of that office and couldn't put the signs up anymore. But by then I had a large email list of people that I was sending pictures of the signs to. And I'd started writing blogs to accompany each inspirational message. Once I didn't have the window, it was easier to just sketch out the week's uplifting message and scan it into the computer for use in the blogs. It felt more friendly and personal than just typing the message into the email. And it was fun to draw a smiley face or

continued...

a flower or some little decorative border around the words. I really enjoyed that part of creating the email "signs." Because I liked it so much, I spent more and more time drawing those embellishments every week. The images I drew to support each message became so elaborate that they began to add – and even expand on – the words themselves. Those joy-filled, hand-drawn signs eventually turned into the coloring book in your hands! I love that my young impulse to say the good stuff has evolved in such a fun, unforeseeable way!

What I love about the format of a coloring book is that it's not just me telling you that you're awesome. It's YOU telling you. Reading positive quotes is certainly wonderful! But using crayons and paper to color in positive statements allows you to receive those messages on whole new levels. You meditate on them. Absorb them. And literally imprint them into your body as well as your mind.

This coloring book reminds you over and over again that you are an extraordinary person! And it invites you to color in those reminders as affirmations of your own brilliant goodness! You get to take matters into your own hands and practice celebrating yourself and life! Coloring itself feels good and is relaxing and fun. Even more than that, when you color these positive statements about yourself and life, you are taking concrete steps toward self-love and expanded thinking! It will encourage you to consider the positive and to say the positive, which will help you create an experience of more possibility and joy!

Have fun coloring, saying and living all that good stuff!

Sky-high thanks for giving me another opportunity to celebrate you, me, and this amazing experience of being alive!

Christina Brittain
October 2015

Feel free to.....

1. Color outside the lines (or not!).
2. Toss out any ideas about what color things are "supposed" to be.
3. Add your own words.
4. Use crayons, pens, colored pencils, pastels, paint, glitter, sequins, stickers, magazine cutouts, feathers....(you get the idea).
5. Draw in extra stuff – a mustache on that flower? Polka dots on that bear?
6. Write journal entries on the back (or front) of the drawings.
7. Color only part of a picture.
8. Skip through the book or go sequentially.
9. Color on your lunch break to relax and reset.
10. Color with friends over a glass of wine – or coffee and cake!
11. Color in silence – or with your favorite music – whatever feels best.
12. Color under your bedspread with a flashlight.
13. Color alone for quiet time or meditation.
14. Color with your kids, your parents, your siblings or your spouse.
15. Make photocopies of pictures of yourself and loved ones, then glue your faces on the figures and objects on the drawings!
16. Mail one to a friend – color it in, or send it blank with some crayons in the envelope.
17. Hang your favorite drawings on the wall of your office, bedroom or kitchen.
18. Take apart the book and hang all the drawings together on a wall. Your own personal oracle.
19. Color in the book together with your family or a dear group of friends. You'll create a special book you can all cherish. Or take each of your colored pages out of the book and hang them up together as a community "quilt."
20. Sing songs while you color.
21. Dance while you color.
22. Do yoga while you color.
23. Light a candle or incense while you color.
24. Read the words out loud to yourself.
25. Enjoy the simplicity of the line drawings and don't color at all.
26. Give yourself every freedom possible – with this book and in life in general!

And away we go...

The Point is to enjoy it!!!

Joy is the point!

Of course you want to enjoy your life!
You just keep forgetting to!
Here's your reminder:
Joy is still right here, right now!
Get back into the habit
of happily discovering everything!
The thrill of a swing set.
A dandelion. Grass. Stars.
Laughter and squeals of delight
are coming from your own heart
and have been all along!
Remember!
You ARE joy.
Life is shining.
Turn your wild child face up to the sun
and grin, grin, grin again!

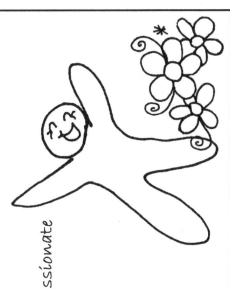

We are life

Life is romping through us!
Galloping in our veins
and pounding our beautiful hearts
and pumping our perfect limbs
in a wild dance of endless possibility and love!
Life watches itself
feels itself
in everything we do
and it rejoices at how limitless, gorgeous and passionate
we are/it is.
Life breathes us
and we make life truly ALIVE!

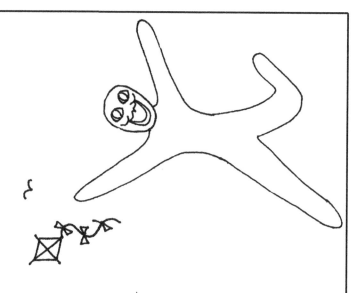

The fullness of life

The ecstasy of living!
The times of celebration too big to contain
so they burst out of us
in rolling laughter
in our dancing, leaping play
in quiet, rapturous tears
and in simple, exquisite hugs...
Whether we catch it like a glint of sun on water
or see it as the whole, flashing, golden sea
the fullness of life
dances before us –
and as us –
every day
and in every single moment!

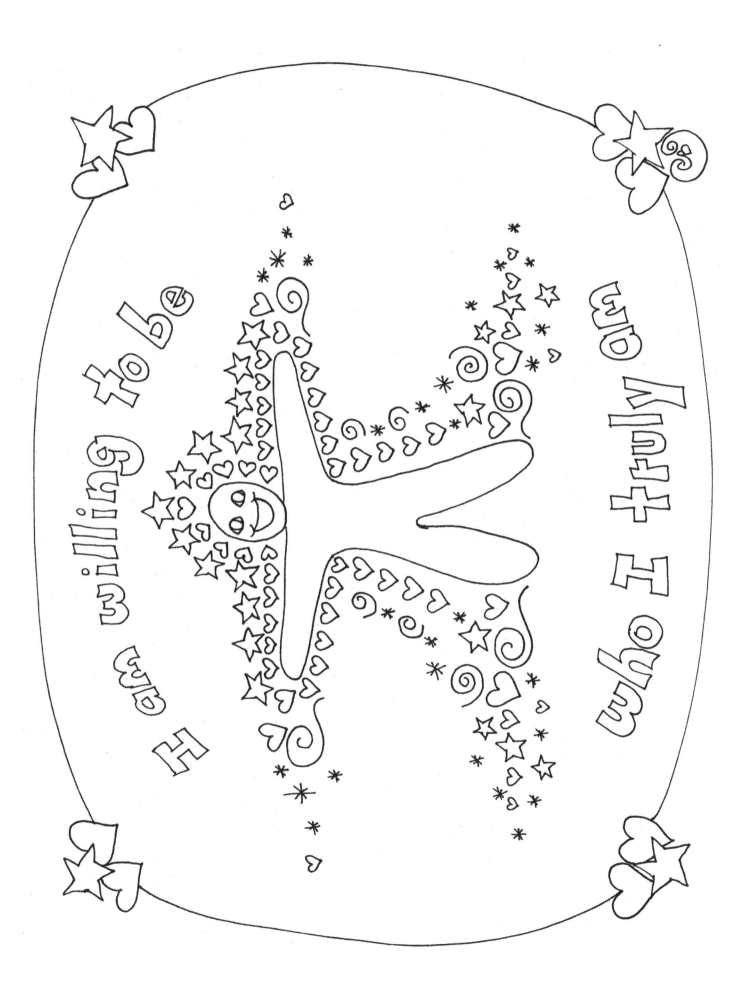

Who you are

You came to this party
wearing exactly that dress because you loved it.
Why would you hide in the bathroom
scrambling to make alterations
so that you look like everyone else?
That's impossible
because everyone else is hiding in corners changing their outfits too –
tearing and re-sewing the minute a new fashion walks through the door!
What a waste of time!
And what a waste of a good party!
Our clothes don't fit us now anyway –
why don't we all drop them
and step out naked to the celebration
shining just as we are!
Laughing, dancing
perfect, precious and unique
as the very day we got our birthday suits.

The beautiful line

You add to Heaven every day.
What you dream, say, touch and move
sends the angels into tailspins of ecstasy!
They clasp their hands with the beauty of it ALL.
And they want to play with you!
If you listen carefully
you can hear Heaven whispering fun ideas in your heart!
New ways of thinking.
New games to play.
New songs to sing
as you run free and radiant
through the lush, green fields of Earth.

You and the universe

You are a wise, powerful being.
You know how to create worlds.
Nevermind the pocket change or new car!

Sit on your throne
with a grin and silly crown
and call the magic!
Feel for who you really are!
When you line up with your truest self
you line up with the universe!
All the doors open
all the paths clear
and from out of the Mystery
whole kingdoms are built for you.
And in you.

Laugh
and let ALL IS WELL rule.
Existence will come running out to play!

Infinite possibilities

All things
came from the limitless, magical No Thing.
You
are made of infinite possibility!
And that's your nature!
The power of CREATION
is vibrating in your cells
and calling your heart to dream into the universe.
Tap into that!
Feel into the stars, worlds and galaxies!
Feel into the endless ocean of YES!
And know that who you are —
and what you imagine —
help existence dance into being.

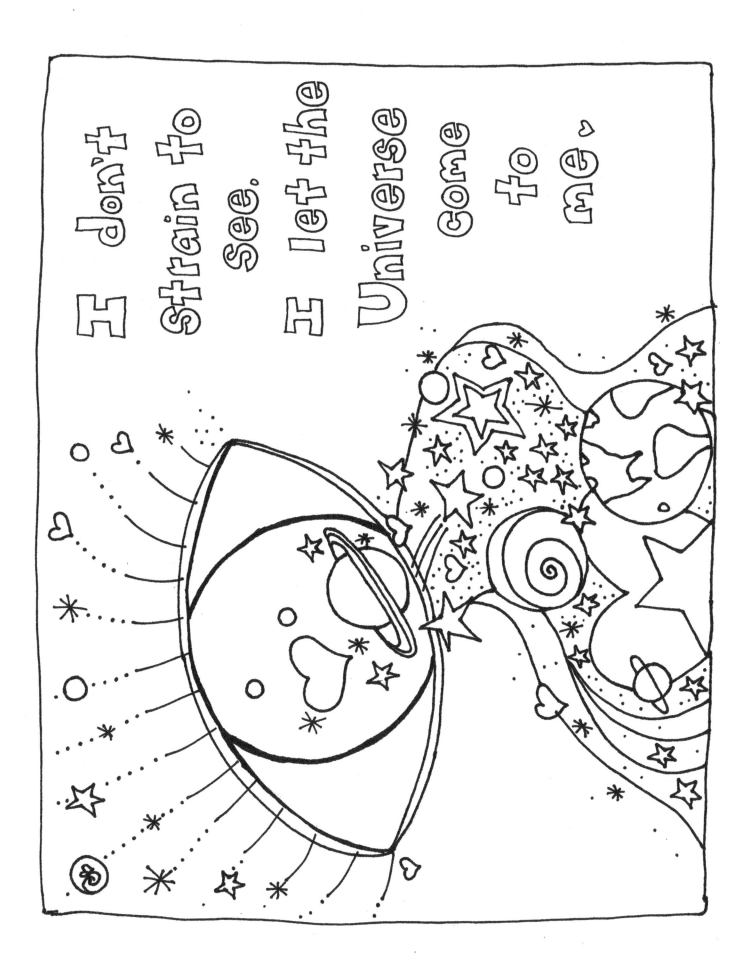

Let the universe come to you

No matter how carefully you choreograph
life is always an improvisation!
Because you are alive and changing!
And so is everything in existence!
Let yourself move with every new moment.
Trust in the loving arms of Mystery.
Surrender to the gorgeous, unplanned twists and turns.
Relax and enjoy, knowing
that the universe and you are exquisite dance partners
the dance floor is limitless
and the steps always unfold perfectly.

It's always perfect timing

Relax!
There is nothing BUT perfect timing.
The universe is THAT smart!

Don't worry
that the ship has sailed
or the train left the station.
That just wasn't your ride
and there's always another!
There is no "should have"
or "too late"
or "need to wait."
Your timing is always perfect.
That's how life –
and you –
are designed!

Chill out!

What if there's actually nothing to figure out?
What if the "problem" is something you're making up in your head?
Time always makes it clear if any action is needed.
And time usually dissolves most problems anyway.
Let all the answers come in their own time –
and they always do
when we get back to enjoying
and chill out!

Lighten up

Are you trying to carry the world
on your shoulders again?
Or trying to control Life
and make it – and everybody in it – behave according to your plan?
Lighten up, will ya?!
The world is carrying itself nicely
Life generally has a better plan than you do
and people get to be in charge of themselves!
Ahh! Look at all the free time you have now!
Get back to the business of enjoying yourself
being kind to yourself
and trusting that everything's working out
juuust fine!

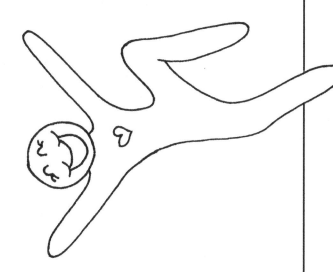

Wheee!

It's okay to have fun!
Your soul came for the joyride!
Not to prove anything or "behave!"
How silly that is to your spirit
that wants to romp and play
touch and taste
and experience this wild, wide world
with glee!!
Keep reminding yourself of this jubilant truth:
You have infinite permission –
and intention –
to enjoy your life!

What makes you feel alive?

Wake up!
You're alive!
You get to go and do and be and feel
all the things that light you up
and open your heart.
You get to EXPERIENCE
the magnificent thrill of Life!
Every rich emotion and sensation is here for you.
And you are here to be alive
as only you can.
What makes YOU celebrate your own aliveness?
Do more of that!!

Think thoughts that feel good

Your mind is your reality.
What you think is what you experience.
Have more fun in there!
Daydream because it's a joy!
Tell more jokes and look for what's funny!
Think kindly toward yourself and others
because it brings you peace and possibility.
Notice the beauty all around you
and linger in your appreciation of it.
Explore what feels good to think about!
Then you can follow your smiling heart
and body
into whole new ways of being.

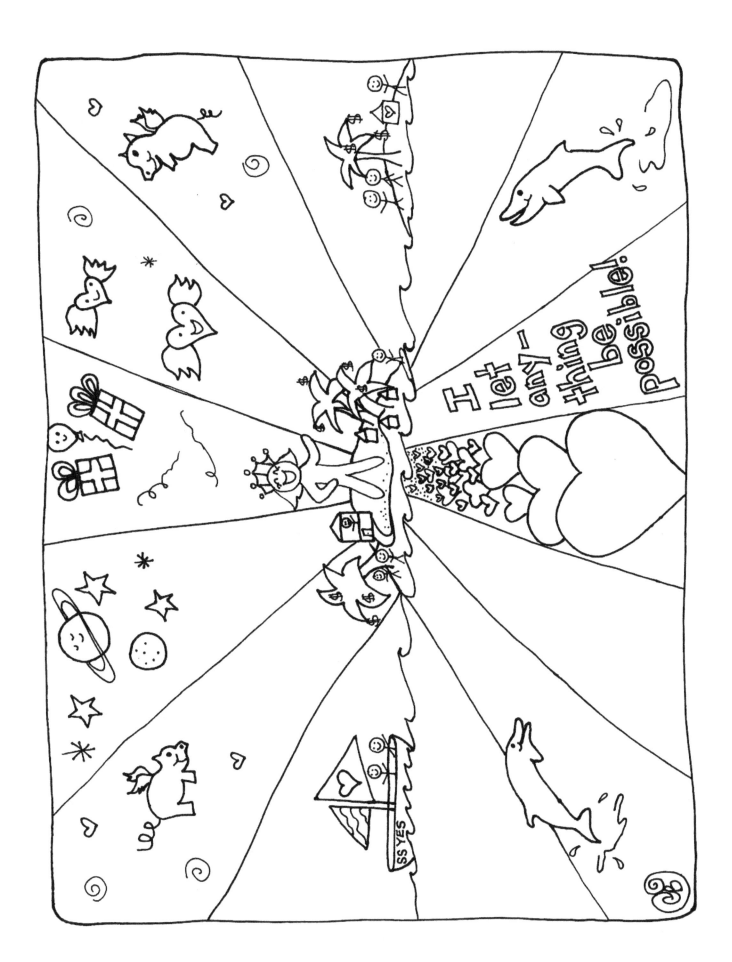

Anything is possible

Pigs flying?
Free reign of your own island?
Being showered with gifts from the heavens?
Why not?
In this limitless universe
anything can happen.
Don't cut yourself off from your infinite nature!
Let yourself dream!
Let anything be possible!

Wouldn't it be awesome if...?

Existence actually organizes
around what we imagine.
Possibility thinking
is a real force for change.
Dream, and you make it possible.
Imagine, and you affect the stuff of the universe!

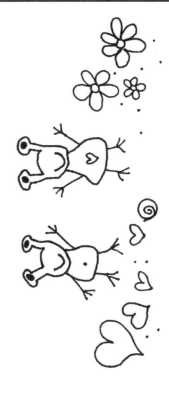

Friendship expands joy and possibilities

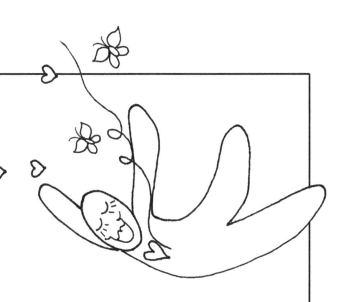

Celebrate friendship!

Thank goodness
we are not all given our own, individual planet to live on!
Well, life is smarter than that of course!
It knows that Everything expands through sharing
and Everything is improved that way too.
So we are designed to love!
We are built to share the world!
Our hearts, minds, ideas and perspectives all grow
through the beautiful gift of human connection!
It's such fun to have playmates!!
Celebrate all your friendships
and all the joyful sharing this world makes possible!

Happy hug

Oh happy is the hug!
The shared joy
and connection of friends!
The warm celebration of life
that the angels are jealous of!
The human embrace
is such a privileged way to rejoice
in this amazing experience of Earth!

Birds!
Flowers!
Sunshine!
Laughter!
Dancing!
And TOUCH!
Oh happy human gift!
Oh beautiful, happy hug!

How do you want to feel?

It happens –
people go on autopilot
and forget that they even WANT to feel good.
Isn't that wild?!
They just accept being sad, bored or numb as normal.
How do YOU want to feel in your life?
The simple, powerful truth
is that when we ask ourselves what we prefer
it automatically brings more of it to us.
No matter what our lives look like
we can FEEL more of anything we choose.
Love. Connection. Satisfaction.
Fun. Interest. Joy!
You can experience your life any way you want!
Don't wait!
You can feel it on purpose right now.

I have the Power of intention

YES YES YES!!

smooth sailing

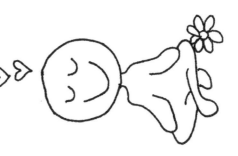

The power of intention

Your body is listening to everything you think!
And it's organized for action!
What you focus on actually changes
your biochemistry, your personality and your perspective!
Choose how you want to feel
and it opens the floodgates for all those awesome emotions!
Decide what you'd like to experience
and it points your whole being in that direction!
You have the power!
Name your intentions!
Not only will your body rush to make it possible –
the whole UNIVERSE will too!

Priority check

Live your life
according to what's important to YOU.
Double check
that you're not spending your time
doing what someone else thinks you should.
And re-evaluate often!
You are changing every day!
Let yourself grow
with love and respect.
Honor and follow your true heart.
It will reward you with energy, fulfillment and passion!
It will always reveal a life you love!

What's my motivation?

Wait - why am I doing this again??

hmmm.....

What's my motivation?

Why are you doing that?

Do you really want to?

Check yourself!

Any chance it's obligation?

Or that you're secretly hoping to get something out of it?

Like approval, for example?

Hey, we all do it!

But if it comes from genuine interest and joy

we don't need any justification or hidden agenda.

We can say or do anything we want

and only what feels right.

Then life is much freer, easier

and WAY more fun!

Seriously?

Ha ha ha ha ha!
You had yourself going there for a second, didn't you?!
Did you forget you are made of Light?
Did you forget that none of the details really matter
when the bottom line is Joy?

Oh right!
litught!

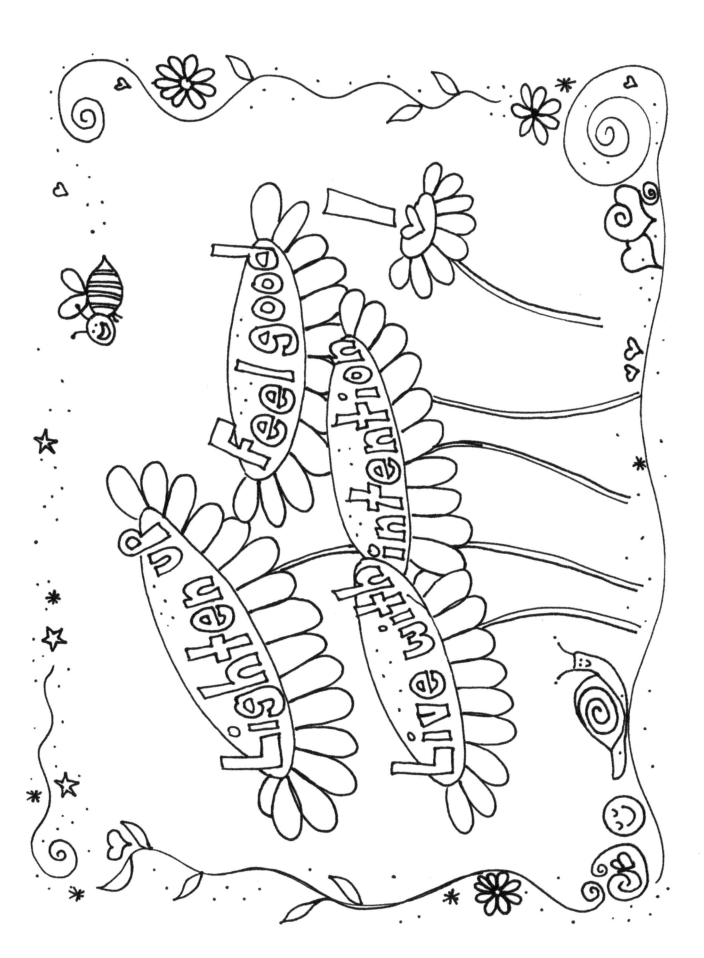

Lighten up. Feel good. Live with intention.

What's important to you?
Once you get clear about that
things get muuuuch simpler!
Stuff that doesn't matter falls away naturally
and it's easy to live happier and lighter.

You don't waste energy
on things you realize you don't care about
which means you have more energy for what you do care about.

You feel better. You feel good.
And knowing what's important to you
you're always gently guided by that.
You effortlessly line up with the life you choose.

You LIVE your intentions.
What's your joyful truth?
What's important to YOU?

New talk, new walk

Begin again!
Why drag that clunky old story along with you?
It has you walking in circles!
That heavy trunk is filled with moth-eaten costumes from a play
you were tired of acting out years ago!
Trade the whole lot in
for traveling clothes!
Free to go anywhere now
start imagining those beautiful, new lands
and begin practicing
those joyful languages –
immediately!

<u>Let it be easy</u>

Struggle is way overrated
really inefficient
and completely unnecessary.
Life is built to flow
and everything's moving along perfectly.
The universe TOTALLY has this covered.
You can relax, trust
and let it be easy!

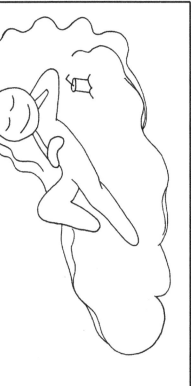

What's your vibe?

What does it feel like to be you?
Close your eyes.
Connect.
Listen to all that you are.
Let every part of you sing!
Then send your truest songs to the universe!
They might be songs of
celebration! satisfaction! confidence! enthusiasm!
or deep love and appreciation
for yourself and others.
What song do you hear inside you?
What song do you choose?
What song ARE you right now?
Let it ring out into All Things!

You are Love

It's in your nature to love
because you ARE love!
Stand in that truth!

Be your loving self
and radiate that joy and light!

Everything you adore will thrive and grow.

Be the love that you are, on purpose!

Here's an invitation:

Name 5 things you love about the world.

Name 5 things you love about anyone you know.

And definitely name 5 things you love about yourself!

Feel-good
DOING comes from

Feel-good
BEING

Feel good

It's not about what you do.
It's about how you feel.
Take the time to feel good.
All your actions will be inspired
and all your doing will be blessed!

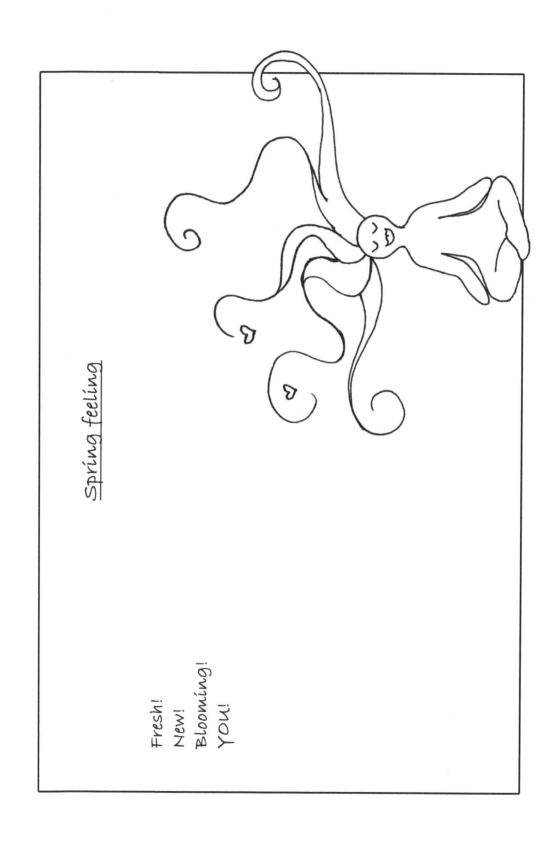

Spring feeling

Fresh!
New!
Blooming!
YOU!

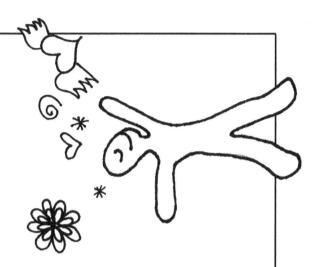

Your joy heals

Suffering in order to help someone else
is no help at all.
Cast off those shackling ideas
that send you against what is right for you
for any reason.
Unchain yourself
and follow your bouncing heart!
What is best for you
is always what's best for everyone else too!
Free, joyful you
romping in the world
brings light
liberation
and beauty
to every corner of the universe
and every being in it.

Trust your gut

Feel free to consult with your mind.
But it's your body that always knows the answer.
Close your eyes
breathe deep breaths
and listen to what comes up from the heart!
Does it feel spacious and free
or tight and constricted when you think about that thing?
Your body knows
and will guide you to all your yeses
by what feels good!

Relax. Sweet. Easy. Simple.

Ever notice how the mind
likes to make things more complicated than they really are?
Relax!
Enjoy the moment!
Move with the natural flow of life.
Sweet.
Easy.
Simple.

Be led by joy!

Tra la la!
Put one happy foot in front of the other!
The path you end up walking
will be richer, clearer

more satisfying, more joyful
and more filled with delightful surprises
than any life you could have planned!
Let joy be your compass
and follow your dancing feet
into the magical unknown!

How good?

Well?
How good CAN you stand it?
Consider that.

Best.
Meditation.
Ever!!!

Life Lover

You have a not-so-secret lover
throwing itself into your arms – right now!
The Divine Lover
is leaving gifts at your doorstep
adoring your every movement
and thrilling at your joy
all day long.
Turn toward the embrace.
Stop pretending to resist!
Melt and surrender
into Life's passionate, tender arms.
Turn inward
and outward
and in all ways
to the Divine romance
that has been courting you
all the days of your life.

Presents

Problems in the future aren't real.
They're just scary stories.
Why worry about something that hasn't happened?
Problems in the past are over.
And we can never be sure we are remembering them right
or that we had all the information then anyway.
Problems in the present are rare.
And even they are gifts in disguise
that we just haven't recognized.
Stay awake to all the presents!
Stay here, now, with open eyes and arms
joyfully waiting to embrace the new blessings in every moment.
Life will fall all over itself with joy
that you are finally letting it give you
all the love, good and wonder your heart can carry —
and more.
Always, always more.

The way to have blessings is to count them!

Blessings

Every day
Life treats you as the royal being that you are.
Treasures are laid at your feet
pleasures big and small arranged for your delight!
Wonders of the world
and miraculous ideas and events
are offered to you with endless cheer
in honor and celebration of your Great Presence.
Wake up and look around your regal bed chamber!
The floor, the walls, the sky, the world
are strewn with blessings and gifts
because you deserve them
because they are your birthright
and because it thrills the universe
to give you every richness and beauty.
Rub your eyes free of sleep
and take in the bounty!

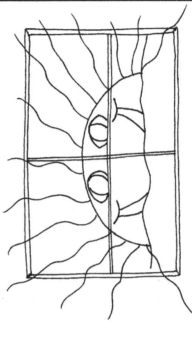

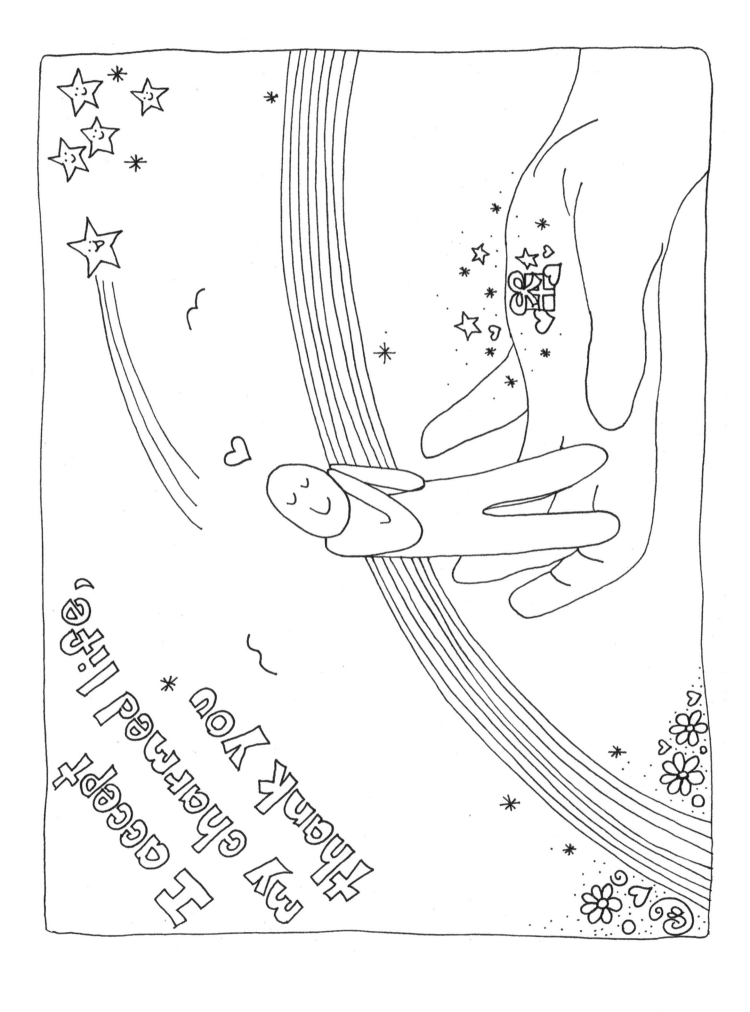

Your charmed life

All you have to do is say yes.
It's right there in front of you.
LIFE IS BEAUTIFUL.
Go ahead – open your mind, heart and arms and let it in.
Everything is happening just for you.
It's all been orchestrated
blessed and charmed
because you are infinitely loved
worthy
and celebrated by All Creation.
Relax. Breathe. Let it be easy.
Receive the sweetness of being you.

Live your beautiful life.

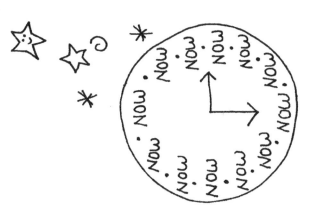

Be happy now!

You may not have heard yet
but happiness is free!
It's available now
and you don't have to pay for it!
Seriously!
No need to achieve anything first
wait for someone to give it to you
or earn it in any way.
Ta da!
No waiting!
All yours!
Be happy now
and because all the nows turn into your life
you're guaranteed a happily ever after.
Pass it on!

And one more thought...

Say the good stuff!

Look around you and really see!
Notice all there is to LOVE!
See it!
Feel it!
Wake up to it!
Then announce the joyful news everywhere!
Anyone and everyone is uplifted
by your loving attention!
And the world is made even better
when you count its blessings.
See it!
Say it!
Sing the praise
from the mountain tops
and you will bring it alive
in your own heart
and in the heart of the whole world.

About the Author

Christina Brittain holds a Masters of Fine Arts in Dance, a Masters level professional diploma in Expressive Arts Therapy, and a wide variety of certifications in energetic medicine. Christina grew up naturally combining arts and energy for personal growth and awareness. One of her earliest memories was of being taken to see a Native American shaman. By age 5, she was drawing, writing poems and dancing to intentionally express her feelings and shift her mood. Today, her inspirational cartoons, intuitive counseling practice, and workshops focus on the conscious use of thought and imagination to create more inner freedom and joy. Christina is the Vice President of The Patrice M. Cox Foundation, which is dedicated to helping people learn how to love themselves. She is also the author of *The Comfort Coloring Book*. Christina lives in San Diego, surrounded by beauty and an extraordinarily wonderful group of friends. You can find out more about her work at www.ChristinaBrittain.com and www.PatriceMCoxFoundation.org.

Printed in the United States
By Bookmasters